First published 2005 by Walker Books Ltd, 87 Vauxhall Walk, London SE11 5HJ

1 2 3 4 5 6 7 8 9 10   © 2005 Caroline Glicksman

The right of Caroline Glicksman to be identified as author/illustrator of this work has been

asserted by her in accordance with the Copyright, Designs and Patents Act 1988

This book has been typeset in Albertus   Printed in China

 This book is for Jessie,
who was a top dog too.

British Library Cataloguing in Publication Data: a catalogue record

for this book is available from the British Library

ISBN 1-84428-018-7   www.walkerbooks.co.uk

BIG BLACK DOG

Caroline Glicksman

WALKER BOOKS
AND SUBSIDIARIES
LONDON · BOSTON · SYDNEY · AUCKLAND

In a town far away lived

BIG
BLACK
DOG.

He was very ...

Whenever he went

for a walk in the park,

everyone ran away.

Big Black Dog was *so* scary that the mayor had made him **Chief Burglar-Catcher.**

But he never had anything to do. All the burglars had left town long ago because they were so afraid of him.

NAME
Big Black
Dog
POSITION
Chief
Burglar-
Catcher

Emmeline's
Teas & Cakes

The Barking Daily

ANOTHER
CRIME-
FREE
MONTH

By Sniffer
Our crime correspondent
Once again, the mayor was at
that there were absolutely n
AT ALL last month in Ken
Super-scary
The mayor said this
showed the success
of his controversial
appointment of su
scary Big Black
Dog as Chief
Catcher.
Read more
and 17-25

Only his friend Emmeline
knew Big Black Dog's secret,
which was that …

...he was
scared of

LOUD NOISES

and
spiders

and
cats

and
strawberry
jelly...

...and even his
own reflection
in the mirror!

NAME
Big Black
Dog
POSITION
Chief
Burglar-
Catcher

But most of all, Big Black Dog was scared
of *ever* having to catch a burglar.

Emmeline tried to help Big Black Dog to be brave by telling him about her adventures, but it only made him feel more scared.

INTREPID
AVIATOR
CONQUERS
ATLANTIC

Pioneering poodle
Emmeline Vester—

Then one morning,
everyone in the town woke up
to find they had been burgled!

The mayor rang Big Black Dog. "The whole town is counting on you to catch the villain," he said.

Big Black Dog was

TERRIFIED.

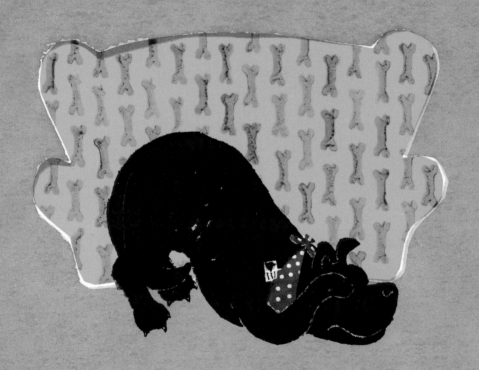

He spent all day
hiding behind the sofa.

RING
RING

When it got dark, he decided to run away.

He wrapped a few of his favourite things
in his scarf and went to Emmeline's
tea shop to say goodbye.

But when no one answered the door,
Big Black Dog knew something was wrong.
Then he heard a muffled bark.
Emmeline was in trouble!

Big Black Dog forced the door open
and quickly rescued his friend.

"Watch out!" gasped Emmeline. **"It's ...**

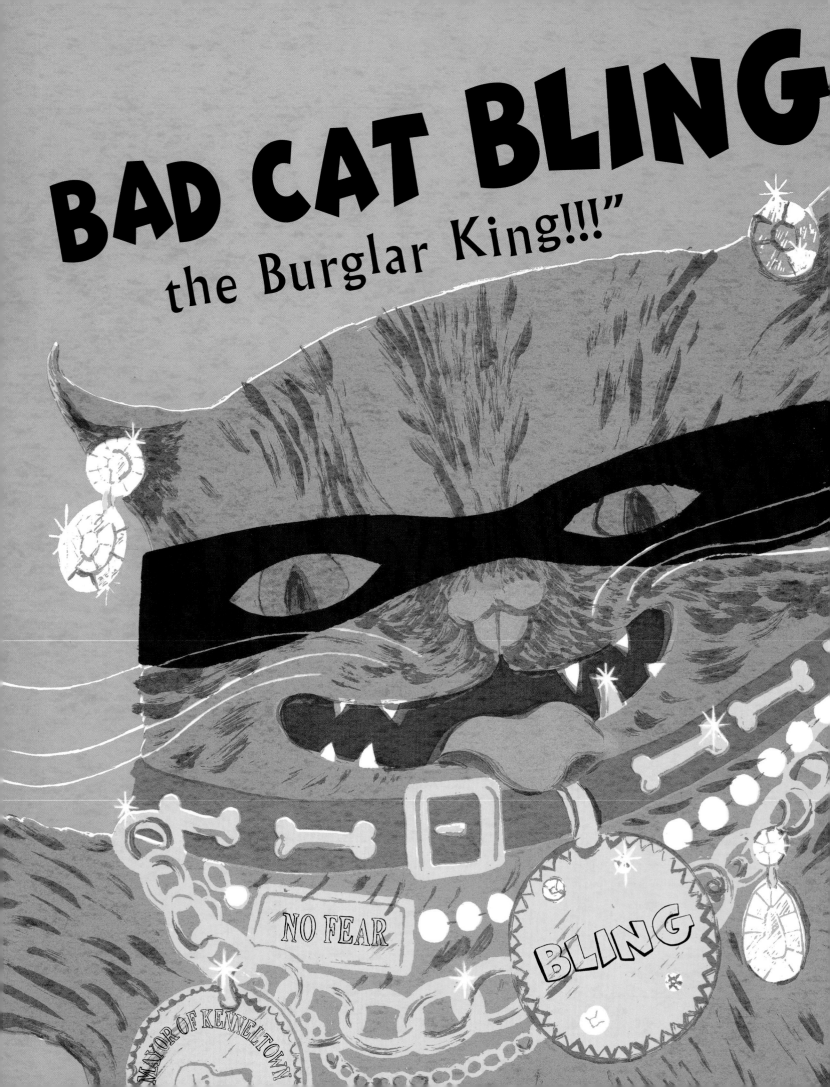

For just a second,
Big Black Dog felt all wobbly
inside. A burglar! A cat!

But then he felt so angry about all
the mean things the burglar had done
that he forgot he was scared and ...

Bad Cat Bling flew up in the air... looped the loop...

...and landed in his very own

SWAG BAG.

Quickly, Big Black Dog phoned the mayor.
"Send round the police," he barked,
"the cat's in the bag."

"Thank you, Big Black Dog," said Emmeline.
"You were so brave!"

But Big Black Dog wasn't
feeling brave at all –
what was that loud,
scary noise outside?

Emmeline ran over
to the window.
"Look!" she said.

A huge crowd was shouting,

TOP DOG! TOP DOG! TOP DOG!

For the second time that day,
Big Black Dog forgot to be afraid.

No one runs away from Big Black Dog any more.
Instead, they call him Brave Black Dog
and he gets invited to lots of parties.

Sometimes he still feels a *little* bit scared,

FOR BRAVERY

NAME
BRAVEBlack Dog
POSITION
Chief Burglar-Catcher

but after all, he says, you can still be brave, even if you feel like a wobbly jelly inside.